The Unicorn of the West

To Virginia Marie, Lauren, and Allison,
who wanted a story of unicorns,
and to Elaine Marie, gratefully
—A.F.A.

For my mother
—A. P.

The Unicorn of the West

by Alma Flor Ada   illustrated by Abigail Pizer

Atheneum   1994   New York

Maxwell Macmillan Canada   *Toronto*   Maxwell Macmillan International   *New York   Oxford   Singapore   Sydney*

Every afternoon, when the sky began to turn red, he came out of the woods. He walked with his fine hooves over the new grass to the edge of the high cliffs. There he watched as the fiery sun set over the ocean.

It was his favorite moment of the day. The rest of the time he roamed the solitary forest. He had never met any of the other creatures who lived there. Often, when he drank the fresh water of a spring that ran among the rocks, he would look in the still waters of a pool. The water returned the image of his face surrounded by his long, floating mane. And because his golden horn reminded him of the fiery sun, he would smile happily.

One morning, when the tree branches had begun to sprout buds, he was surprised by a new sound. First he imagined that it was the wind rustling among the trees, but since he had never heard the wind sing like this before, he searched to find where the sound was coming from.

At last he saw a small creature perched on a branch and looking right at him.

"Hello!" he said. "Who are you?"

"I'm a robin," answered the bird.

He was curious. "How do you know that?" he asked.

"How could I not know?" replied the robin. "My mother is a robin, my father is a robin, my brothers and sisters are robins, my uncles and aunts and all my cousins are robins. And who are you? I've never seen anyone like you before."

"I don't know," he answered. "My horn is golden like the sun, and my mane is as white as the clouds. But I'm not the sun, and I'm not the clouds. I don't know who I am."

"I'll keep flying to see if I can find someone just like you, so I can tell you who you are," said the bird. And before he flew off, he added, "Good-bye, Friend."

For many days the long-maned animal listened attentively for the robin's return. But all he heard was the wind rustling among the branches and the constant pounding of the sea.

One summer day, as he ran through a meadow studded with flowers, he was very surprised to see one of the flowers begin to fly.

He rushed to get a closer look at this new wonder. And he discovered that it was not a flower, but a creature with wings as light as petals, shining brightly in the sunlight.

"Hello," he greeted the winged flower. "Please wait and tell me, who are you?"

"I'm a butterfly," answered the butterfly, landing on a flower.

"How do you know that?"

"How could I not know?" answered the butterfly. "My mother was a butterfly, my father was a butterfly, and my hundreds of brothers and sisters are all butterflies. Who are you? I have never seen anyone quite like you before."

"I don't know," he answered. "My horn is golden like the sun, and my mane is as white as the daisies. But I know I'm neither sun nor flower." And then he added sadly, "I don't know who I am, but a robin once called me Friend."

"I will fly as far as I can, to see if I can find someone like you to tell you who you are," said the butterfly. And as she flew away she added, "I'll see you soon, Friend."

For many days he watched the meadow, hoping to see the butterfly return. But although new flowers burst open among the grasses, none left their stems to fly.

Soon the leaves began to turn gold and crimson. One afternoon, while he drank from a spring, he was surprised to see another face reflected in the water—a furry face with sharp, bright eyes.

He turned his head and saw a small animal with a bushy tail looking at him from a nearby tree trunk.

"Hello!" he greeted the furry creature. "Who are you?"

"I'm a squirrel," said the squirrel, twitching his tail.

"How do you know that?"

"How could I not know?" answered the squirrel. "My mother is a squirrel, my father is a squirrel, my three brothers, my uncles, and my cousins are all squirrels. My grandparents were all squirrels. And who are you? I have never seen anyone quite like you before."

"I don't know," he answered. "My horn is golden like the sun, and my mane is as white as sea foam. But I know that I'm neither sun nor foam." Then he added, "I don't know who I am, but a robin and a butterfly once called me Friend."

"I'll keep traveling. Perhaps I will find someone like you so that I can tell you who you are," said the squirrel. And as he jumped to the next tree, he added, "See you soon, Friend!"

And so from that day he waited to hear the song of the robin again, to discover the butterfly in the meadow once more, or to see the lively face of the squirrel among the trees. But all he heard was the sound of the wind in the trees and the pounding of the waves against the cliffs. And when he looked at himself in the pool, all that he saw was his own face and the reflection of the leafless branches of the trees.

One full-moon night he heard a new sound echoing from the mountains. It was not the sound of the wind nor the sound of a storm. It was neither the song of birds nor the music of the rains. It was a melody both far and near, sad and happy, lively and slow.

The melody seemed to ask him to follow, and so he did, his light mane floating like night clouds beneath the full moon. He left the meadow and entered the woods, crossing one river and two streams. As the moon disappeared now and again behind clouds, he crossed a valley by the light of the stars. By the time he arrived at the foot of the mountains, the sky was turning pink.

Suddenly it seemed that his own reflection was walking toward him through the early morning mist. The same golden horn, the same light mane appeared not once, not twice, but three times, in front of him, on his right, and on his left.

But these reflections were alive. They were beings just like him—the same agile legs and sharp hooves, the same long, floating manes and brilliant eyes.

"Thank you for answering the call of the music," said the one who had appeared on the left.

"We could not fail to keep this meeting," said the one in front.

"But who are you?" he asked, gazing at them in awe. "And why are we here?"

"Once every seven years, we gather here on the first full moon after the winter solstice," said the one on the right.

"This is our way of making sure that there is enough love for all in the world," said the one in front.

"And that beautiful dreams live on," said the one on the left.

"But who are you?" he asked again. "And who am I?"

"I am the Unicorn of the North," said the one who had appeared on the left. "I live in the land of ice and snow. Since my coat is the color of snow, no one has ever been able to see me. Those few who have seen my horn thought they saw a ray of sun glinting off the ice."

"I am the Unicorn of the East," said the one who had come from the direction of the rising sun. "I live among desert sands. Not many cross the desert, so very few have ever seen me. And those who did thought they saw a mirage."

"I am the Unicorn of the South," said the one on the right. "I live in the middle of the jungle, where monkeys swing from branch to branch and lions roar at night. No one knows that there is a unicorn in the jungles of the south, since falling leaves cover all my tracks and the thick brush does not let anyone see what is hiding among the trees."

"And I, then? Who am I?"

"You are the Unicorn of the West," said the Unicorn of the North.

"You come from the direction of the setting sun," said the Unicorn of the East.

"Since you are so young, this is the first time you have met with us," added the Unicorn of the South.

"I am the Unicorn of the West," he repeated slowly to himself.

At sunset the unicorns said good-bye.

"We will come together again in seven years," said the Unicorn of the North as he left toward the land of ice and snow.

"On the first full moon after the winter solstice," said the Unicorn of the East. And he headed off to sand dunes and an oasis with date palms.

"To be sure that the world is filled with love," said the Unicorn of the South as he left for the jungle of tall trees and fragrant orchids.

"Until we meet again," said the Unicorn of the West. And he started his journey home, toward the high cliffs by the sea.

When he arrived at the meadow, the squirrel came to meet him.

"Friend, I now know who you are!" she chattered. "I traveled to the land of ice and snow, and there I saw someone just like you."

Just then the robin flew in.

"Friend, I now know who you are!" he sang happily. "I flew all the way to the desert, where few things grow. There, in a small oasis, I saw someone just like you."

With a flutter of wings, the butterfly drew near.

"Friend, I found out who you are!" she said softly as she danced in the breeze. "I flew deep into the jungle, and there among the trees I saw someone who looks just like you."

"I know now that I am the Unicorn of the West," said the Unicorn, tossing back his shining mane.

And then, looking at each one of them, he added:

"But I would like it very much if you kept calling me Friend."

Text copyright © 1994 by Alma Flor Ada
Illustrations copyright © 1994 by Abigail Pizer

Atheneum
Macmillan Publishing Company
866 Third Avenue
New York, NY 10022

Maxwell Macmillan Canada, Inc.
1200 Eglinton Avenue East
Suite 200
Don Mills, Ontario M3C 3N1

Macmillan Publishing Company is part of the Maxwell
Communication Group of Companies.

First edition
Printed in the United States of America
10 9 8 7 6 5 4 3 2 1
The text of this book is set in 16 point Belwe Lt.
The illustrations are rendered in watercolor.

Library of Congress Cataloging-in-Publication Data

Ada, Alma Flor.
The unicorn of the west / by Alma Flor Ada.—1st ed.
p.   cm.
Summary: A robin, butterfly, and squirrel try to help a mysterious
animal find his identity.
ISBN 0-689-31778-6
[1. Unicorns—Fiction.   2. Identity—Fiction.   3. Animals—
Fiction.]   I. Title.
PZ7.A1857Un 1994
[E]—dc20   92-7425

Printed on recycled paper